THE DUKE OF SYCAMORE

Written and illustrated by Edgar Parker

Five strange friends wished to visit the King. Although they knew only noblemen were allowed in court, they set out through the forest to the castle. They weren't quite sure what they should say to the King, if they were ever in his presence. They made quite a procession indeed. The Mouse was his Grace's locksmith, with lots of keys. The Owl and the Rabbit were the bearers of his Grace's sedan chair, on which sat the Squirrel, the Duke of Sycamore. The Frog was the minstrel. The masquerade was delightful, until the King wished to return the visit and the Duke had no castle in which to return his hospitality. They were all in a fix and how they solved this problem involves one of the most hilarious hoaxes of all time.

* * *

Classification and Dewey Decimal: Fiction (Fic)

About the Author and Illustrator:

EDGAR PARKER, was born in Meridian, Mississippi, where he attended college. He specialized in art at the University of Alabama and then came to New York to study painting, etching and engraving. Mr. Parker lives in New York City and because of his interest in animals, makes regular visits to the local zoos.

The Duke of Sycamore

EDGAR PARKER

1965 FIRST CADMUS EDITION
THIS SPECIAL EDITION IS PUBLISHED BY ARRANGEMENT WITH
THE PUBLISHERS OF THE REGULAR EDITION
HOUGHTON MIFFLIN COMPANY
BY
E. M. HALE AND COMPANY
EAU CLAIRE, WISCONSIN

This edition lithographed in U. S. A. by Wetzel Bros., Inc., Milwaukee 2, Wisconsin

ONE DAY a bobwhite saw a strange procession coming toward him through the forest. A mouse, carrying a heavy ring of keys, led the way. Then came an owl and a rabbit, supporting between them a large, elegant sort of box, in

which sat a squirrel. Last of all came a frog, dancing about and singing.

"What is this?" the bobwhite asked.

"I am His Grace's locksmith," said the mouse.

"I am His Grace's minstrel," said the frog.

"And we are the bearers of His Grace's sedan chair," said the owl and the rabbit.

"His '*Grace*'! — What is *that?*" exclaimed the bobwhite.

"That," the squirrel replied grandly, "is how one speaks

of dukes, duchesses and arch-
bishops. I — am His Grace the
Duke of Sycamore. I'm going
to court and see the King."
The bobwhite bowed very
low, and the procession went
on its way.

"He believed us!" whispered
the mouse.

"Sh-h-h," cautioned the rabbit — for, to tell the truth, the
squirrel was not a duke at all,
nor were the others his serv-
ants. They were merely five
friends who had wished for
a long time to go to court
and see the King. They had
been told, however, that only
noblemen were allowed at
court, and it had taken them
many weeks — and all their
savings — to equip themselves
as they imagined a duke and
his attendants would appear.
The squirrel had embroidered

a laprobe to present to the King; surely, they thought, this would please the King so much that — even if their masquerade were discovered — he would not be angry.

"He believed us!" the mouse whispered again, when the bobwhite was no longer in sight.

"Yes," replied the owl, "but then he's probably never seen a duke before, so how should he know? He might believe you if you told him you were a hippopotamus — or — a bandicoot."

"Oh!" the mouse squealed in delight, "*do* let's go back and tell him I'm a hippopotamus. I should like ever so much to be mistaken for a hippopotamus — just once!"

"You should be satisfied as it is," the owl answered gruffly. "The King will not be so easily fooled — you can be sure of that."

This set them all to worrying again, and the squirrel asked the owl, "What must I say when introduced to the King?"

"Oh, he will ask you 'How are you?' or something like that; and you should reply 'Very well, thank you.' "

"Is that all?"

"Well, you might ask him how *he* does. But perhaps you'd better not; that might seem too inquisitive."

And the squirrel began to murmur over and over to himself, "Very well, thank you — very well, thank you — "

4

Suddenly a fierce, yellow-eyed, murderous, ravenous, gluttonous, voracious and ill-natured lynx leaped into the path and, before his paws had touched the ground, the owl, the frog, the rabbit and the mouse leaped into the bushes. But the squirrel had no time to escape from the sedan chair; he closed the windows, and drew the blinds, while the lynx walked around and around him.

"Well, well, what's this?" the lynx said, licking his lips.

The squirrel thought he'd better reply, and in as brave a voice as he could manage he. answered, "The Duke of Sycamore."

"I'm glad to see you; indeed I am! I said to myself, just this morning, 'Now, what I'd like for dinner today is a *duke!*' "

"But a duke isn't good to eat at all," came the trembling voice from the sedan chair.

"Well, if a duke isn't good to eat, I'd like to know what he is good for!"

The squirrel could think of no reply to this. And the lynx began to turn the sedan chair this way and that, wondering how he might open it.

Finally the squirrel said with great positiveness, "A duke tastes like jellied eels, pine cones and broken crockery, all rolled into one."

"Splendid! Splendid!" growled the lynx, giving the sedan chair a vigorous shake. "If there's anything I like it's jellied eels, pine cones and broken crockery, all rolled into one."

"But I'm going to visit the King; he will be very angry if you eat me!" the squirrel cried desperately.

"Well! Going to see the King, are you! I'll tell you what I'll do: I'll let you go see the King. You and your friends — who aren't very sociable, by the way — you ought to come back lots fatter after you've been eating with the King; and

I'll be waiting — right along here — or maybe a little farther on — or maybe a little farther back; but I'll be waiting." And off he went, leaving the sedan chair upside-down.

After making certain that the lynx had really gone, the "duke's" companions returned, and set the chair aright. "My gracious!" sighed the squirrel; but he was too glad to see them again to sulk because they had deserted him.

"Sing us a song, minstrel," he said; "Sing a song about courage, to cheer us." The frog rolled his eyes and muttered, "Courage, courage, courage; let's see now. Ah, I have it!"

"There lived a dragon long ago.
(But first I think you ought to know
That none of this is really so;
   I tell it just for fun.)
This dragon was a fearsome beast,
With fangs three inches long at least.
From north to south, from west to east,
   He frightened everyone.

8

Sharp talons glittered on his toes,
And fire came out his mouth and nose;
Black clouds of smoke and ash arose,
  And smutted up his brow.
A creature always vanished when
It ventured near the dragon's den.
(But there were no real dragons then
  And certainly none now.)
So fearful was the dragon's roar
The sound would rattle every door
For fifty miles around or more.
  (But this is just a tale.)
At last a hero came along.
He said, 'I will avenge this wrong,
Although the dragon's big and strong,
  While I am small and frail.'

A sword, a shield, a trumpet horn,
— All secondhand and slightly worn —
A plume, a banner — ragged, torn —
   Were all he could afford.
He stood before the dragon's cave.
— Was ever anyone so brave! —
A blast upon his horn he gave,
   And waved aloft his sword.
With slippery, swift and silent crawl,
The dragon POUNCED! (But please recall
That none of this is true at all;
   It's meant for your delight.)"

— "No! No! No!" cried the others, quite overcome with alarm. "We don't want to hear it! — Sing another song!" And they set down their burdens, and covered their ears.

   "Well, to be brief — the hero slew
   The dragon with a stroke or two,
   Which, even if the tale were true,
      Would make it end all right."

Just as the song ended, the turrets of the King's castle rose into view, high above the treetops. "Look!" they cried. The towers and the fluttering banners thrilled the little animals. But as they neared the castle they became less brave. A

moat surrounded the walls, and — unless the drawbridge was lowered — there was no way to enter. Now that their journey was over — now that the King's castle stood before them — their courage left them altogether.

"Well, we can't enter," the mouse said, grinning to hide his fear " — and that's that."

"No, no," replied the squirrel, "there's a bell: all we have to do is ring it." But no one stepped forward.

"I expect the King has hundreds and hundreds of lap-robes," sighed the rabbit.

"Let's go back home again," whispered the mouse, so softly — for he was ashamed — that the others mistook it for their own thoughts.

At last the frog closed his eyes, held his breath, and grasped the bell cord: CLANG! CLANG! CLANG! The sound alarmed them all. The mouse dropped his keys and would have run away if the rabbit had not put his foot upon the mouse's tail.

A small shutter opened, and a cat's face appeared in the window. He gazed a long while at each of them. Then he asked, "Well?"

The little beasts stood silently — their hearts pounding — until the frog nudged the owl, who was to be their spokesman.

"The Duke of Sycamore — " the owl began; but in his fright he forgot the rest.

" — wishes to pay his respects to the King!" shouted the frog.

The cat blinked his eyes, and twitched his whiskers once or twice. Then he closed the shutter. With a great clatter and creak of chains, the drawbridge descended over the moat. And they marched into the castle.

The cat greeted them before a large door. He beat a drum; he blew a trumpet; he rapped the doorknocker — and shouted, "The Duke of Sycamore — to pay his respects to the King!" — which was altogether too much for the mouse, and it was all the frog could do to prevent his fleeing.

The sound of much shuffling, bumping and scrambling was heard before the door opened — for the King and his courtiers had been sprawled upon the floor playing marbles, and they could not immediately find the King's crown. But when the visitors entered the room the crown sat upon the King's head, and the King sat upon the throne with all the dignity of one who had never sprawled upon the floor in his life.

The owl and the rabbit set the sedan chair before the throne, and the squirrel stepped out. The King was much larger than they had imagined. The "duke" and his friends exchanged a look of distress; each was thinking the same thought: The laprobe would scarcely cover one knee of the King. But there was no help for it now.

The squirrel bowed, and waited for the King to ask him how he was. But the King only stared at him with the keenest interest. At last, without a word, the squirrel extended the robe before him.

The King whispered to the fox, who stood beside him, "What is it? What do I do with it?"

"Well," answered the fox, "at least you take it, and say 'Thank you'; that much I know." But, as the King bent forward to accept the offering of the trembling squirrel, several dozen marbles escaped from the folds of his clothing and rolled over the floor.

"They're MINE! They're every one MINE!" shouted the King frantically as the courtiers scurried after the marbles. Then composing himself again, he said to the "duke," "Thank you; it is very pretty."

"It is to hold Your Majesty's marbles," the squirrel replied.

"O-o-oh!" cried the King in delight. And with the help of his courtiers he collected the marbles in the laprobe, tied the top with a golden thread, and hung it from his belt. In

the meanwhile the squirrel, having done all he knew to do, re-entered the sedan chair, and when the King looked up from his gift his guests were on their way out.

"Wait! Wait!" he called, "Surely you can stay a while! I'll declare a holiday; we'll have feasts and fireworks, while we become acquainted."

"Why is it," he asked, when the squirrel had returned to the throne, "that you've never come to court before?"

The "duke" glanced anxiously at his friends, but none of them could help him. "Oh, I've been busy, busy, busy," he replied.

"*Everyone* is *always* busy!" the lion said peevishly, and without waiting for an answer he announced loudly, "A holiday — in honor of the Duke of Sycamore!"

There were games every day and banquets every night. One day they put rowboats with red awnings in the moat, and rowed around and around the castle. One night the mouse performed a soft-shoe tap dance on the table, between the gravy boat and the sugar bowl, which pleased the King very much. But he was even more delighted when the frog sang:

> "*The terrapin turtle of Zanzibar,*
> *He rode a tricycle and smoked a cigar.*
> *He sang to himself, as he traveled afar,*
>   '*Oh, where is the bride for me?*'
> *He met a young lizard, a sweet, gentle maid.*

He bowed and saluted, and compliments paid.
He sang her love songs, as they sat in the shade
    Of a blossoming apple tree.
She said, 'This is pleasant, and you are polite;
But how do I know that you never will bite?'
The terrapin answered, 'You don't, and I might.'
    The lizard replied, 'I refuse!'
The terrapin turtle's a bachelor still.
He sings, as he swims in the rollicking rill,
'It is better this way; I can bite when I will,
    And whomsoever I choose.' "

Once the rabbit and the mouse overate, and suffered a severe stomach-ache, notwithstanding which they both declared that they'd "do it all over again."

At length the "duke" and his followers decided that it would be prudent to leave while their masquerade was still undiscovered.

"Oh, it's been such fun!" the rabbit sighed sadly.

But no one had enjoyed the occasion more than the King. And when the frog, at his request, sang "The Terrapin Turtle of Zanzibar" for a last time the King actually wept. They said good-bye continuously for two and a half days before the King consented to their leaving, but it finally seemed the visit had come to an end. And the "duke" and his attendants were fairly over the drawbridge when they heard the King calling "Wait! Wait!" As he overtook them, they saw that he carried a wicker basket, into which he had thrown three oranges, a wooden spoon, a tennis racket, half a mincemeat pie, a pair of galoshes and a change of linen. "You see!" he cried, his face radiant with joy, "I'll simply go with you, and visit your castle for a while."

"Oh dear!" gasped the squirrel. "*My* castle?" — for the fact of the matter was that the squirrel and his friends lived in a hole at the foot of a tree.

The courtiers were fast upon the King's heels. "But Your Majesty can't leave like this!" they cried. "You've just finished one holiday — things have to be put in order first —

and, besides, *we* want to go too, when you visit the duke's castle!" ("Oh dear," the squirrel sighed. "*My* castle!")

"Very well, spoilsports," the King said sullenly, "I'll come back; I'll set the affairs of the kingdom in order; and then — " He turned to his new friends. "By the way, how shall I find His Grace's castle?" ("How, indeed!" muttered the owl.)

"Oh, there are signs all along the way. Your Majesty can't miss it," the frog replied, for the squirrel seemed to have fainted, and something had to be said.

The King stood upon the drawbridge, and waved as long as the little caravan was in sight.

"Oh, oh, oh," whimpered the rabbit, "what shall we do?"

"Obviously, we must leave the country," the owl replied, "and go into hiding before the King discovers that there is no castle — no duchy — no Duke of Sycamore, and furthermore, that there never has been. Oh, oh, oh!"

A CRICKET sat upon a stump at a fork in the path. "What is this?" he asked. "I've never seen such a parade! Why are you so gaily dressed — and yet so sad?"

"Ah," the frog replied, "we are five foolish creatures who have made a bad mistake."

"But where are you going?"

"Away — far away; it matters very little where."

And then — "OH!" they all cried at once, for in their despair they had forgotten, until that very moment, the lynx who lay in wait for them. And, leaving the cricket much puzzled, they set off hurriedly down the strange path. "Wherever this leads us," said the squirrel, "we can meet nothing more terrible than the lynx."

How far they had walked they neither knew nor cared when suddenly they found themselves before a strange castle. And on the door was fixed a sign:

gONE honeY HuntiNg
WILL retUrn IN tWo
mayBe THreE weEks
oR MAYbE lonGeR

—tHE
bEar

"I think he's been gone much longer already," the frog remarked, for the castle seemed quite deserted.

"Look," whispered the rabbit, "the door's ajar." In fact it had nearly fallen from its hinges.

Inside the castle cobwebs hung in every corner. The little animals made tracks in the dust as they roamed about the rooms. "I don't think he's ever coming back," the squirrel whispered. "If only we were sure —."

On the stairs they met a big black beetle. They would have asked him about the bear, but he shrieked and fled when he saw them. In a closet, high in a tower, they found a crane, sitting on a most uncomfortable-looking nest made of old chair rungs, newel posts, bent forks and spoons and at least one weathervane. To their questions the crane would say only, "If nobody bothers me — I bother nobody. Close the door behind you as you leave."

After they had explored all the rooms, they began to whisper among themselves: "Suppose — Perhaps — Do you think — "

And they quickly set to work. They dusted, mopped, mended, polished, painted, scrubbed and swept from the top

of the castle to the bottom — except for the crane's closet.

Once she called out crossly, "This is the *noisiest* house in all the world!" Another time she came down the stairs, and, speaking more civilly, asked them to reserve for her nest any "interesting-looking rubbish." But, otherwise, she didn't interfere.

When the castle was bright and shining inside and out, the rabbit trotted down the path, placing signs along the way: "To THE DUCHY OF SYCAMORE."

The squirrel was baking gingerbread, the owl and the frog

were rehanging the last tapestry, and the rabbit had just re-turned when the mouse ran down from the watch tower. "They're coming!" he cried. "I heard the drum, and the cat is shouting 'Make way for the King!'" At this they scurried madly about, finishing their preparations.

BOOM da-da-da BOOM da-da-da BOOM went the drum. "Make way for the King!"

"Should I greet them on the steps?" asked the squirrel. But there wasn't time: Bam! Bam! Bam! went the doorknocker. "HIS MAJESTY, THE KING — TO PAY HIS RESPECTS TO THE DUKE OF SYCAMORE."

The owl flung wide the door, and the little hosts bowed to the floor. "Ah," said the King, "I smell gingerbread!"

The fun began anew: feasts and frolics, and frolics and feasts.

"Come now," the King said, as they sat down to their fifth

banquet, "it's time we dropped ceremony; you may call me 'Leroy the Tenth.' What may I call you?"

"Mostly, I'm called Squirrel," the "duke" replied — which was quite true, and — until then — he'd never needed any other name. But it was evident that the King was disappointed.

"His Grace's full name," broke in the owl, "is Benjamin — Struthious — Appendage."

"Benjamin *Basil* Struthious Appendage," the frog added.

" — the Twenty-seventh," continued the rabbit.

"Oh, how nice !" cried the King. "Do I have my choice of all those?"

"Yes," answered Benjamin Basil Struthious Appendage the Twenty-seventh. "In fact, you may add to it, if you like."

"I will call you Struthious, then," the King announced. "And I will add to it, too. I appoint you Custodian of the King's Nightcap, and furthermore declare you to be — an Honorary Lion!"

All the court cheered loudly; they weren't a bit jealous, although he was the only Honorary Lion in the kingdom.

"Leroy the Tenth," said the Honorary Lion, "you have been too generous toward me already; but there's a further favor I would ask."

"Only name it!" said the King. And the squirrel asked that each of his companions be given a title or two.

The King was delighted to do so, but he had only time enough to declare the rabbit to be the Baronet of Rodentia when —

An enormous bear stood in the doorway. On his shoulder he carried a barrel of honey. Such was his surprise to see the change that had come over his home (for he had never so much as swept the floor in his life), and to see the many creatures gathered there, that he was speechless.

"Oh, oh," whispered the mouse, "what are we going to do now?"

The squirrel thought quickly. "Ah, there's the honey we've been waiting for," he announced bravely. "Take it to the kitchen, Aleck, and then — go away — please."

At this, the bear roared so furiously that the little beasts fled beneath the King's robe. "Surely," said the "duke" in a quivering voice, "surely my servant has gone mad!"

And, indeed, the bear seemed so. He stamped his feet, gnashed his teeth, roared, raved, and shouted that it was *his* house; it was *his* honey; his name *wasn't* Aleck; and he would *not* go away. It was very easy to believe he had gone mad.

But a lion can roar much louder than a bear. In fact, the King and all his court roared together, and rose from the table, and — if the bear had not fled from the castle there's no guessing what would have happened!

No sooner had the King returned to his seat and all become quiet again than another voice was heard from upstairs: "THIS IS THE NOISIEST HOUSE IN ALL THE WORLD!"

"Now, what is *that?*" exclaimed the King.

With trembling hands the squirrel dipped his handkerchief into a goblet of water, and patted his forehead. "I don't hear a thing," he said. "Sing a song, minstrel — quickly!"

The frog was trembling too, and at first his voice was a faint whisper. He cleared his throat, and began again:

"One day I came upon a snail.
I thought that I would eat him.
But he had vanished head and tail,
And I could only greet him:

'Oh, lovely snail, why do you hide?
Let's talk — with your permission.'
'Speak on; I hear,' the snail replied,
'Quite well in this position.'

'But don't you find it dark and damp?'
I asked him most politely.
'And don't you suffer with the cramp,
To stay wrapt up so tightly?'

'I've plenty room,' the snail replied.
(I think he told a story.)
'And all my needs are here supplied:
A tub and lavatory:

'A chair, a churn, a cedar chest,
And potted plants aplenty;
Some books to read, a bed for rest,
And candles — four and twenty.'

30

And there was more he had to say
Of why his life was merry,
But, as he spoke, I walked away,
And ate a huckleberry."

When the song was finished, the King and his courtiers had forgotten the bear's intrusion and were merry again. Glorious titles were given to the mouse, the owl and the frog, and everyone went to bed happily.

At last the time came for the King's departure. "Oh, it's been such fun, Struthious, that I can't bear the thought of leaving." Tears glistened in the King's eyes. Then his face brightened with delight — "In fact, I don't think I shall!"

"But Your Majesty!" the courtiers cried, "we *must* go; there is so much business — !"

"Very well," the King agreed sadly. "Ah, Struthious, I expect you think I can't manage a kingdom. I can. I do it very well. I don't like it at all, but I do it. You should be glad that you're only a duke, a custodian of my nightcap and an honorary lion, instead of a King."

At this moment the King was very much surprised to see a gawky crane stalk down the stairs and into the room with three gangling and downy baby cranes. She paused at the front door long enough to shout, "I will NEVER come back here again!" And leading her babes before her, she slammed the door.

"What was *that?*" gasped the King.

"That was His Grace's laundress," the owl replied.

"It seems, then, that she has resigned?"

"Yes," said the squirrel, "it seems so."

"Well, now," continued the King, "what was I saying before?"

"Your Majesty was saying good-bye," said the courtiers.

"Was I — really? But I suppose I must. Here, Struthious," said the King, taking the golden chain from his own neck and laying it before the "duke," " — for you. And, in addition, here is my royal banner, which you may fly from your tower, to show all who pass that a great friend of the King lives here."

While the lion was biding farewell to the squirrel in this manner, the owl, the mouse, the frog and the rabbit whispered together: "Do you suppose that we might leave a long letter for the bear, explaining everything?"

"No, no, there shan't be time for that; even now, I expect, he is somewhere very near — watching and waiting."

"OH!"

"OH!"

"OH!"

"As soon as we have put the King out the front door, we must run as fast as we can out the back, and not stop until we are far away."

"OH!"

"OH!"

"OH!"

"Good-bye, Struthious; come to see me very soon."

"Good-bye, Leroy the Tenth."

And then the King and his courtiers were gone; the door had closed behind them; the little beasts were alone. Swiftly they ran through the castle, the squirrel dragging the golden chain behind him, to the back door, where —

— the bear stood waiting!

In an instant he trapped them in a corner. His shoulders heaved with the fury of his breathing; his eyes gleamed; he ground his fangs; he snorted; he snarled; he gurgled; he growled: "Now, I have you!"

"But we cleaned your house!" the rabbit cried.

Nearer and nearer came the bear.

The mouse could stand it no longer; he sat upon the floor and covered his face with his hands. "Go ahead!" he sobbed, "Eat me! Eat me!"

The squirrel stepped forward and, dragging the golden chain, he ran and laid it at the bear's feet. Then he scurried back to his friends.

The bear looked back and forth from the chain to the frightened little animals. "For you!" they cried. "And now we'll go away."

"And never come back."

"We *promise!*"

Frowning, the bear picked up the chain. He attempted to

fasten it about his neck, but his clumsy paws could not manage it.

"If you will kneel," the squirrel suggested timidly, "we will clasp it for you."

Although the bear tried to appear still angry, he thought the chain the most beautiful thing he'd ever seen. Without a word, he knelt and bowed his shoulders. The squirrel and the frog scampered onto his back, and in a moment the chain was fastened.

"Let us tell you all about it, " said the rabbit.

And when everything had been explained, the bear made them tell it all over again. "Oh!" he cried in delight, "I wish I could have been with you! Stay with me; promise me that you'll stay and share my castle, — for, to tell the truth, I'm not only untidy, I'm lonely."

"Then you forgive us?" the mouse asked.

"I forgive you," said the bear.

And that is the end. The King's banner waved from the tower, and so constantly did they and the King visit each other that they often met on the road. Moreover, when it had been explained that he had "recovered his senses," the bear was properly introduced to the King, who promptly bestowed upon him the title of Baron Bismuth.

As for the wicked lynx: he waited, and waited, and waited, — which only served him right.

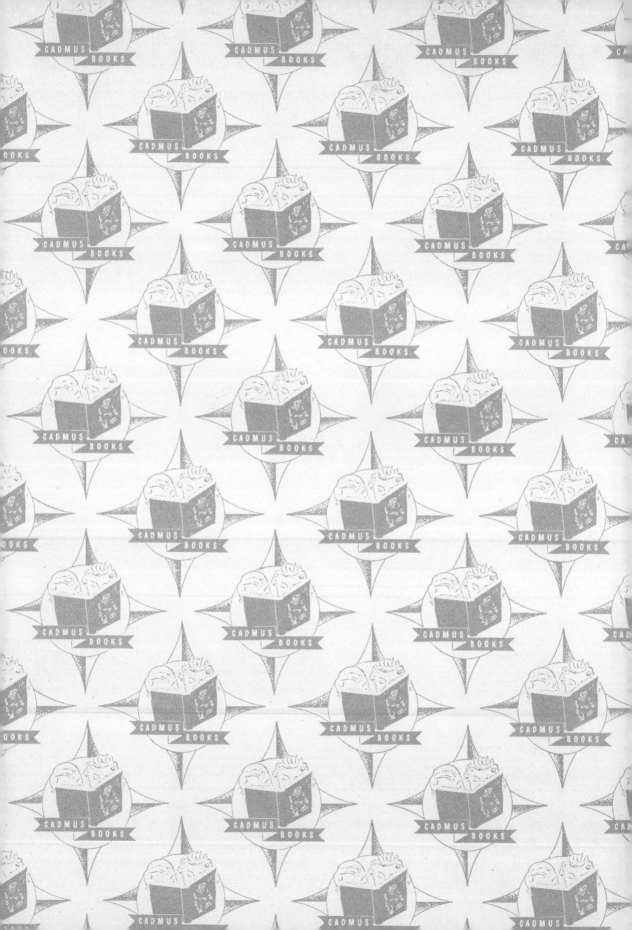